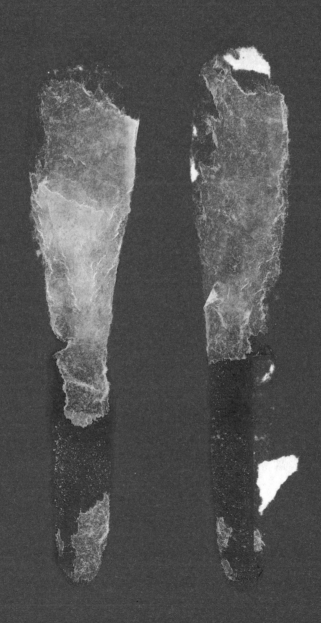

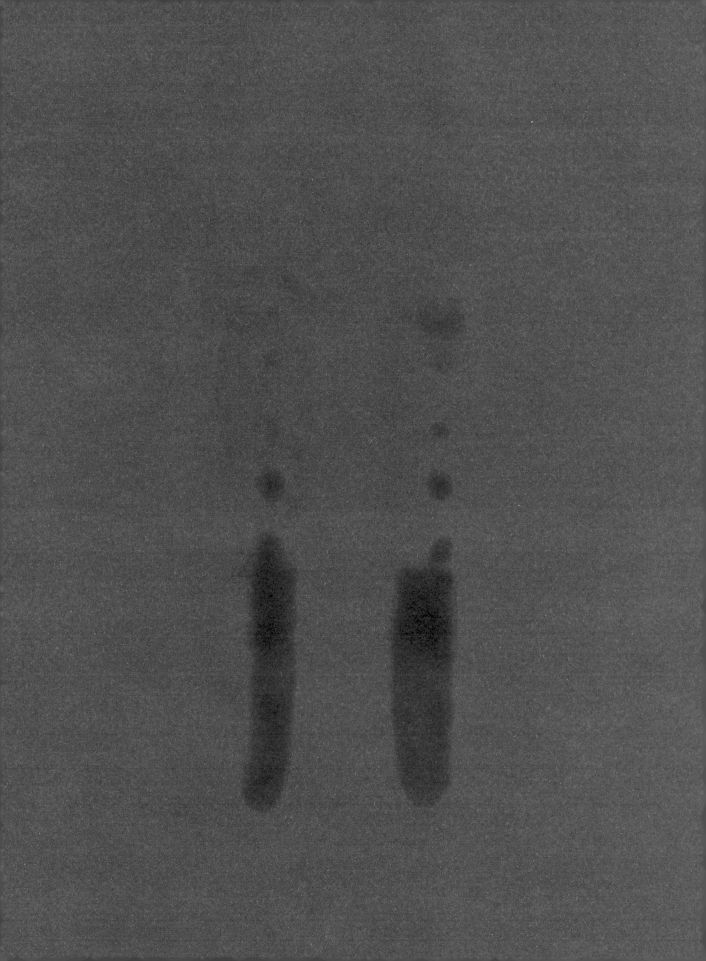

One Giant Leap

ODYSSEY

*To Mom and Dad, for teaching me that imagination
is the best entertainment* —D.M.R.

To Bryan and Barry —T.B.

Copyright © 1996 Trudy Corporation, 353 Main Avenue, Norwalk, CT 06851,
and the Smithsonian Institution, Washington, DC 20560

Soundprints is a division of Trudy Corporation, Norwalk, Connecticut.

Book design: Alleycat Design Inc. New York, NY

10 9   8   7   6   5   4   2
Printed in Hong Kong

Library of Congress Cataloging-in-Publication Data

Rau, Dana Meachen, 1971–
    One giant leap : The first moon landing / by Dana Meachen Rau ;
illustrated by Thomas Buchs.
        p.   cm.
    Summary: While on a field trip to the National Air and Space Museum, Tomas imagines
himself as Neil Armstrong, who was the Mission Commander aboard Apollo 11 and the first
man to set foot on the moon.
    ISBN 1-56899-343-9 (hardcover). — ISBN 1-58899-344-7 (pbk.)
    [1. Project Apollo (U.S.)—Fiction. 2. Moon—Exploration—Fiction. 3. School field trips—
Fiction.] I. Buchs, Thomas, ill.   II. Title
PZ7.R193975On 1996
[Fic]—dc

                                                            96-15035
                                                               CIP
                                                                AC

One Giant Leap

Written by Dana Meachen Rau
Illustrated by Thomas Buchs

Soundprints
Where Children Discover...

Tomas stares impatiently at his watch. "We won't have time to touch the moon rock!" he mumbles to himself.

On the first floor of the National Air and Space Museum, Tomas paces back and forth while his friends, Lucy, Kevin, and Emma, fumble with the museum map.

"We'll go to the planetarium first!" Emma tries to take charge, neatly folding up the map.

"Hold on!" Kevin snatches it from her hands. He has his own ideas.

"I want to touch the moon rock!" Tomas pleads. But his friends are arguing too loudly to hear.

5

"What's the use!" Tomas shoves his hands in his pockets and wanders to the exhibit at the end of the hall.

"Actual Apollo Lunar Module," Tomas reads the sign. "This is just like the ship that brought the first men to the moon!"

"Tomas!" his friends call.

"His head's in the stars again," Lucy giggles.

Tomas doesn't hear them. He stares at the lunar module's silver and gold frame. "Wow! Imagine being the first man to walk on the moon!"

"Neil! Neil!" Someone taps Tomas on the shoulder. He is no longer at the museum. Around him now are over 600 switches and dials. *Where am I?* he wonders. Then he looks down. He is wearing a bulky space suit with the name NEIL ARMSTRONG stitched on the front!

Tomas spins around as if he were swimming.
It feels like there is no gravity! Two men are beside him.
He recognizes them from his books in school—Buzz
Aldrin and Mike Collins, the Apollo 11 astronauts.

"Are you ready, Mission Commander?" Aldrin asks
Tomas.

Aldrin and Collins are pushing buttons and flipping switches all over *Columbia,* the command module.

It must be July 20, 1969, Tomas realizes. He looks toward the pointed end of *Columbia,* where the landing module, *Eagle,* is attached. *Eagle* will soon begin its historic descent and, in just a few hours, it will touch down on the moon.

"Time to power up," Aldrin says, as he turns dials on the console.

"But I'm not Armstrong!" Tomas's pleas are drowned out by the voice of Mission Control crackling over the radio—from 240,000 miles away! He has never been this far from home.

"I'm only a ten-year-old boy!" It's too late. Tomas has already been ushered into *Eagle* and buckled tightly next to Aldrin. The hatch snaps shut.

Tomas looks back at Earth, hanging in the black sky like a giant blue marble. At least Aldrin can't see Tomas's palms sweating nervously under his gloves.

Tomas almost wishes he were staying with Collins, safe in the command module, orbiting 70 miles above the moon until Tomas and Aldrin return. Tomas's heart pounds as *Eagle* backs slowly away from *Columbia*.

"*Eagle* has wings!" Tomas shouts over the radio. *But let's hope it can fly*, he thinks to himself as they head for their landing site on the moon—the flat plains of the Sea of Tranquillity.

"I can do this," Tomas whispers to himself. "After all, the computer controls our landing. All I have to do is sit back and watch."

Suddenly, after only five minutes of powered flight, the digits 1202 flash in alarm on the computer display. Aldrin reports it to Mission Control.

"What's a 1202?" Mission Control radios.

"They don't even know!" Tomas panics.

Aldrin figures out that 1202 means the computer is overloaded. Tomas stares as *Eagle* speeds toward a crater as big as a football field and filled with rocks as big as cars!

What should we do? Tomas worries. He looks over at Aldrin, but he is too busy checking the computer display to even notice the boulders outside the window.

If the computer can't pilot Eagle *over the rocks, then the Mission Commander has to,* Tomas thinks. *And since Armstrong is Commander, and I'm Armstrong. . .*

Tomas grips the controls *. . .then I have to!*

I can do this, I can do this, Tomas repeats to himself.

Armstrong is a pilot, and has even flown in space before. I hope some of Armstrong's training is in my head somewhere!

Eagle skims over the top of the boulder field, and Tomas searches frantically for a clear landing site. *Wow! This is just like a video game,* Tomas thinks.

But all he sees are rocks. Tomas steers *Eagle* left. The fuel gauge is plummeting down.

Then, just beyond the next crater he spots a smooth, level place about 200 feet square. "I found it!" Tomas yells. On one side it is bordered by craters, and on the other by boulders. He'll have to be careful. And their descent fuel is getting very low—only enough for 30 seconds more flight!

Suddenly, the engine kicks up an enormous cloud of dust that engulfs the ship. Tomas straightens out *Eagle*. He can't see how close they are to the surface. *Eagle* feels like an elevator going down. He closes his eyes. They are going to crash!

Then—*plop*. They land on the western edge of the Sea of Tranquillity.

That's it? Tomas thinks. It doesn't feel like they've really landed. Aldrin is even checking the touchdown sensors to be sure.

A big smile stretches across Tomas's face. He did it! He grabs the radio. *I should let Mission Control know we're okay,* he thinks. "Houston, Tranquillity Base here. The *Eagle* has landed."

According to the flight plan, Tomas and Aldrin are supposed to take a four-hour nap before leaving *Eagle*, to be rested in case they need to make an emergency lift off.

"But I haven't taken a nap since I was little! I want to go now!" Tomas complains. Aldrin and Mission Control agree. After all, everyone is eager to see them walk on the moon.

Tomas still has some waiting to do. It takes them four more hours to prepare, depressurizing the cabin and suiting up into the three layers of the special space suits. Once the heavy backpacks holding their portable life support systems are secure, they open the hatch.

Tomas gasps with wonder. *Eagle* has landed on a wide, level plain, scattered with rocks and boulders and dotted with craters, some as big as 30 feet wide! The surface is chalky gray and reminds Tomas of a desert. Except there is life on a desert. Here Tomas is an alien, visiting a strange new world.

Tomas clicks on the camera mounted to the side of *Eagle*. Now he's really nervous, because 600 million people on Earth are waiting to watch him on television!

Backing down *Eagle's* ladder, Tomas hops down to the metal landing pad.

He lifts his right boot and plants it on the moon's dusty surface. *It's like cocoa powder,* he thinks to himself. Then he bounces up and down. Because the moon has only one sixth of the earth's gravity, Tomas feels like a rubber ball.

He almost lifts his other foot. *Oops! Better not take another step before I say Armstrong's famous words!* Tomas chuckles. He clears his throat and proudly declares to all the people listening, "That's one small step for man, one giant leap for mankind."

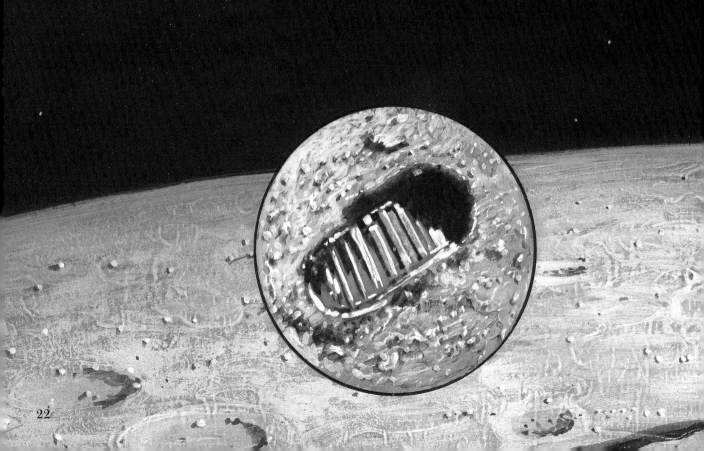

Tomas springs across the moon's surface like a kangaroo.
"I can jump so far!" he smiles. "And in slow motion!"
    Soon Aldrin joins him, and it is time for their first priority,
to collect moon rocks. Tomas grabs his aluminum scoop and
searches for samples, like he's digging for lost pirate treasure.

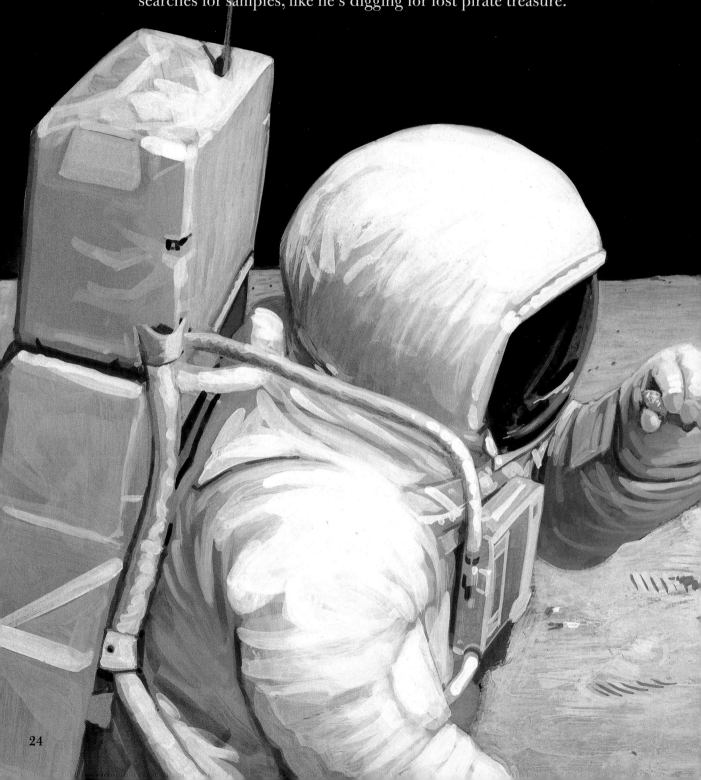

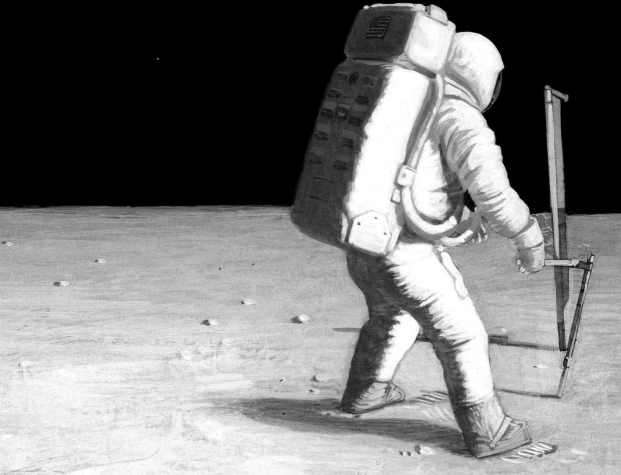

He scoops up a pile of rocks and watches as half of them scatter into the distance like pieces of popcorn. But he does manage to catch one in his glove.

It is light gray, like the rest of the colorless surface. A small piece is chipped away, and inside he sees it is very dark, almost black.

He picks up more specimens and carries them over to *Eagle*. Soon the rock-boxes are full.

After Tomas and Aldrin set up three lunar experiments for the scientists on Earth, Mission Control tells them they can stay on the surface an extra fifteen minutes. It isn't much more time, but enough for Tomas to do some quick exploring.

The crater he flew over just before they landed is close enough. Tomas hops to the edge of the pit.

It looks like a huge empty swimming pool, about 80 feet across and 20 feet deep. He starts to climb over the edge to explore the bottom for rocks.

Wait! Tomas thinks. *What if I get stuck? Aldrin is too far away to save me!* Instead, he takes a few pictures with his special space camera and returns to the landing site.

Tomas and Aldrin spend their last few minutes outside on the moon's surface taking samples of the rocks right around *Eagle's* base. Tomas has been outside for almost three hours, but now it is time to climb back up the ladder and take off.

Tomas gazes once more at the moon's curved horizon. He doesn't want to leave. There is still so much more to explore!

Tomas! Tomas!" Lucy calls to him. "If you want to see the moon rock, we'll go there first."

Tomas turns to her, confused. He's back at the museum. Dazed, he looks down. He is a ten-year-old again, wearing jeans and not a space suit.

"Let's go see it!" Tomas runs ahead. He wants to show his friends what a moon rock looks like. After all, he has already held one in his hand.

About the First Moon Landing

In 1961, President Kennedy challenged the American people to land a man on the moon before the end of the decade. In 1969, the Apollo 11 astronauts met the challenge. The flight of Apollo 11 was one of the most widely followed events in human history. It is estimated that 600 million people (about one fifth of the world's population) watched at least part of the historic journey on television.

Launched atop a mighty Saturn V rocket, three men—Neil Armstrong, Edwin (Buzz) Aldrin, and Michael Collins—set out on their journey on July 16, 1969. Four days later, the lunar module *Eagle* separated from the command module *Columbia* and began its 12-minute descent. On July 20,1969, first Neil Armstrong and then Buzz Aldrin had the honor of being the first men to step onto the surface of the moon.

On the moon, the astronauts' main goal was to collect rock specimens and set up scientific experiments. But they also scheduled time to take pictures and erect an American flag. (It took them many tries before it would stand up straight!)

The journey to the moon was not an easy one. It took the skill and dedication of thousands of men and women. Thanks to their expertise and care, even the most dangerous maneuvers (among them, leaving Earth's orbit, landing and taking off from the moon, docking with the command module while orbiting the moon, and reentering Earth's atmosphere) were accomplished precisely as planned. On July 24, 1969, the astronauts in *Columbia* splashed down safely in the Pacific Ocean. Safe aboard the aircraft carrier *U.S.S. Hornet,* the astronauts were congratulated by an excited and admiring world.

A plaque left on the moon by Armstrong and Aldrin stated simply: Here Men From Planet Earth First Set Foot Upon the Moon July 1969 A.D. We Came In Peace For All Mankind.

The lunar landing was an inspiration. Mankind could accomplish what at first seemed impossible. In the words used by Neil Armstrong as he made his historic first step, it was truly "one giant leap for mankind."

Glossary

Apollo 11: one of the 17 Apollo flights that focused on moon landing and exploration

command module: the spacecraft that takes the astronauts to the moon, orbits the moon while the astronauts explore its surface, and brings the astronauts back to Earth

depressurize: to reduce the pressure inside a spacecraft to a similar level found outside, so the astronauts can safely adapt to their new surroundings

gravity: the force that draws all bodies toward the center of a mass and gives them weight

horizon: the line in the distance where the sky appears to meet the land

lunar module: the spacecraft that disconnects from the command module and is designed specifically to land on the moon's surface

Mission Commander: the astronaut in charge of the mission with the authority to abort the mission if necessary

Mission Control: the base of operations, located in Houston, Texas, where technicians and scientists control and monitor the operations of the spacecraft

planetarium: a model or representation of the solar system and the night sky, designed to teach people about outer space

Sea of Tranquillity: the landing site on the moon chosen for the Apollo 11 astronauts, due to its flat landscape

specimen: a sample of material studied by scientists

touchdown sensors: the part of the spacecraft that lets the astronauts know they have landed safely